the sun came out,
the sky turned blue.

When you were born
the snow melted,

the birds sang,
the flowers grew.

When you were born
the grass sighed,

the ocean sparkled,
a breeze blew.

When you were born
our hearts sang,

our spirits soared,
our troubles flew.

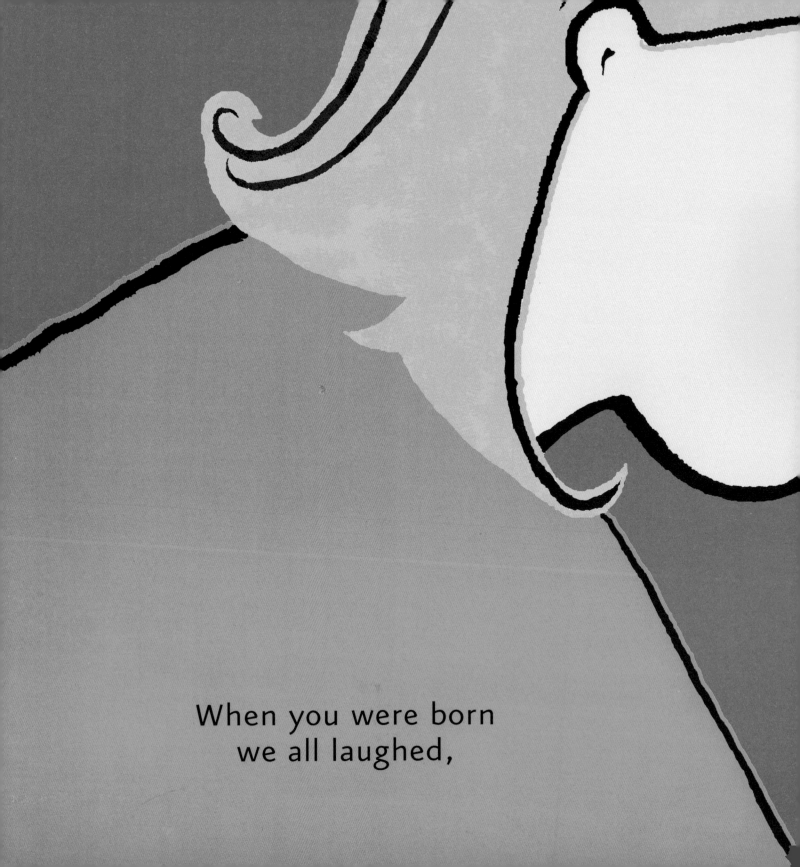

When you were born
we all laughed,

we all cried,
our dreams came true.